T0248329

GREEK GODS
and *Goddesses*

I AM ARES!

WRITTEN BY
THOMAS KINGSLEY TROUPE

ILLUSTRATED BY
FELISHIA HENDITIRTO

TABLE OF CONTENTS

A Mermaid Book
SEAHORSE
PUBLISHING

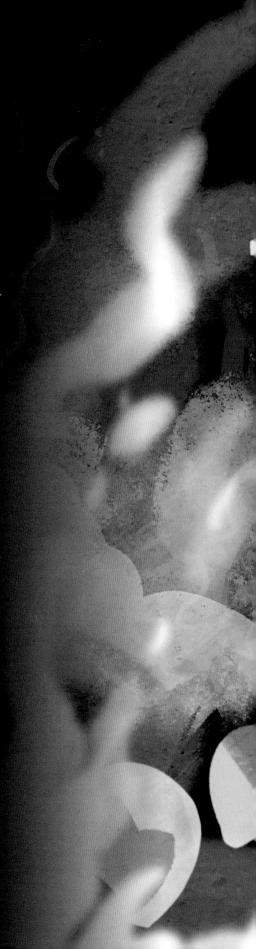

Hey, little one! Do you want to fight?

It wouldn't be a good idea on your part. There's no way you'd win. For I am Ares! Everyone knows me as the ancient Greek god of war and violence. That's right, you don't want to mess with me!

Sure, there are other Olympian gods out there. But none are as fearsome as me, Ares: GOD OF WAR. I am always seeking battle and bloodshed and will stop at nothing for victory.

It's true that my love for a good brawl has made me less popular among the other gods. Who cares? Let me tell you my story.

I am a son of Zeus. Oh, you've heard of him? He's the king of all Olympian gods. So, it makes sense that I'm pretty great and powerful. He and my mother, Hera, argue about how I was born. Hera says Zeus isn't my real dad!

Hera says that since Zeus had a daughter without a mother, she wanted to have a son without a father. So Khloris, the goddess of flowers and nymphs, made Hera touch a magic flower. The flower made her pregnant, and I was born. Lame! I'm not sure I believe that.

Whether Zeus was my father or whether I was created from some dumb flower, I'm still pretty awesome. I'm one of the most important immortal residents of Mount Olympus. From up there, our family once ruled the world.

  There were twelve of us living on Mount Olympus.
First, we have Zeus and Hera (Mom and Dad). Then,
my uncle Poseidon and my aunts Demeter and Hestia.
Finally, my brothers and sisters: Athena, Apollo,
Artemis, Hephaestus, Dionysus, and Aphrodite. Oh,
and me, of course.

Did you know Mount Olympus was attacked? Yep, and it was my relatives who did it.

My cousins Otus and Ephialtes were hunters who became giants. Otus wanted to be with my sister Artemis. Ephialtes really liked my mom, Hera. They had a plan to kidnap the goddesses.

To reach Olympus, they piled mountains on top of each other. From the top of the stack, they tried to storm the home of the gods.

I couldn't let them get my mom and sister. I did all I could, but they somehow defeated me. They wrapped me in chains and put me in a bronze urn. Then, they left me on the island of Naxos.

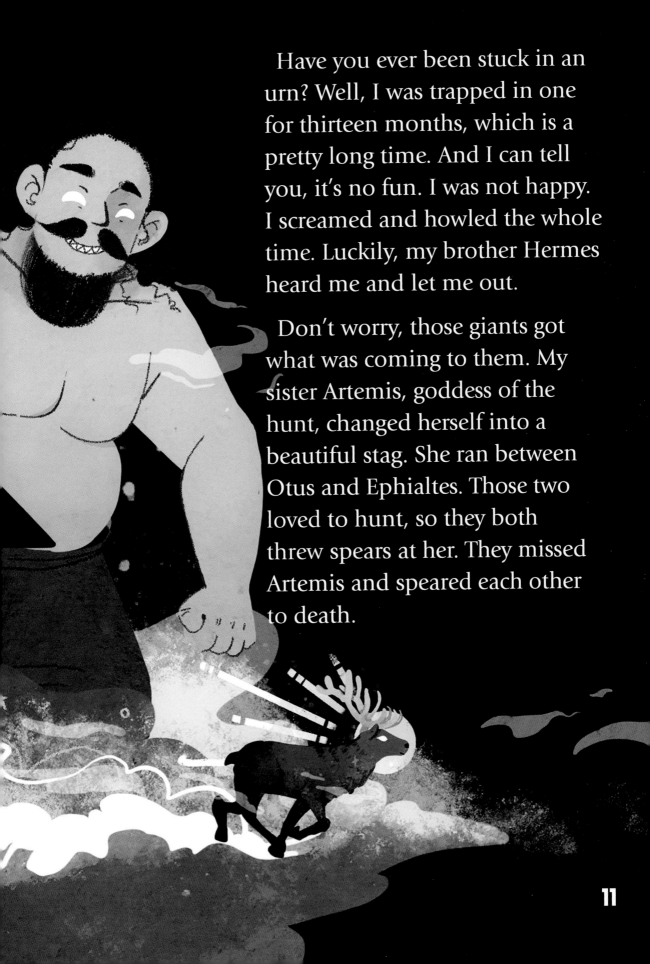

Have you ever been stuck in an urn? Well, I was trapped in one for thirteen months, which is a pretty long time. And I can tell you, it's no fun. I was not happy. I screamed and howled the whole time. Luckily, my brother Hermes heard me and let me out.

Don't worry, those giants got what was coming to them. My sister Artemis, goddess of the hunt, changed herself into a beautiful stag. She ran between Otus and Ephialtes. Those two loved to hunt, so they both threw spears at her. They missed Artemis and speared each other to death.

Relationships are tough among the gods of ancient Greece. My brother Hephaestus was married to Aphrodite, the goddess of love. Lucky guy.

Well, I really liked Aphrodite…a lot. I guess she liked me, too. We decided to sneak away together.

Hephaestus was the god of fire, blacksmiths, and metalworking. Nice guy. He even made me a great spear or two. He was always busy in his workshop at night, so he didn't know that Aphrodite and I were spending time together behind his back. Sorry, Heph.

I'm not the only one who noticed Aphrodite. Turns out some good-looking guy named Adonis liked her, too. Adonis was the son of Theias, King of Assyria. Lots of girls had a crush on him.

I found out that Aphrodite actually liked Adonis as well! They were in love. I wasn't happy.

Just like my dumb giant cousins, Adonis liked to hunt. Aphrodite warned Adonis not to go too far into the forest during his hunts. Of course, he didn't listen. One day, all alone and deep in the woods, Adonis came across a wild boar.

This boar was something else. It kept running at Adonis and trying to attack him. No matter what Adonis did, the boar would not leave him alone. Finally, when Adonis had his guard down, the boar charged at him with its nasty tusks.

The tusks pierced Adonis and killed him.
He was so far into the forest that no one
could hear his cries.

You'll never guess who that wild boar was.
That's right, ME! I turned myself into a
boar to teach Adonis a lesson. That's what
you get for messing with the god of war!

Sadly, my relationship with Aphrodite didn't last. Hephaestus found out about us and captured us together in an invisible net. All the other gods came over to see us and said mean things. Finally, we were released and had to go our separate ways.

I did end up having children of my own. Lots of them! Alcippe was one of my daughters. My cousin Halirrhothius, son of Uncle Poseidon, attacked her. I found out about it and grew furious. I grabbed my spear and killed him on the spot.

I was put on trial for the murder of Halirrhothius. Some of my fellow gods came to judge my crime. When they learned all the facts, I was found innocent. Even so, killing the son of a god is a serious offense. The court said I must be punished.

I was made to work as a slave for a year. One year for Greek gods is about eight years for you shrimpy little mortals. It wasn't easy work, but it made me stronger and even meaner than before.

Okay, okay. That should do it. I don't want to give you nightmares.

There is more to tell, but I think you've learned enough about my mighty history. I hope that if you ever hear about a battle or fighting or bloodshed, you think of me.

Never forget my name, weak one. I am the god of war. I am ARES!

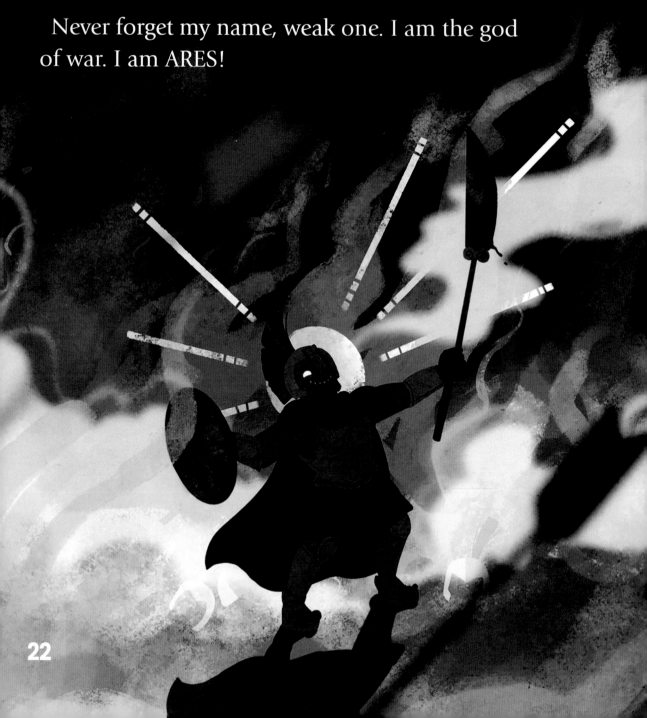

What Is Greek Mythology?

Greek mythology is a collection of epic stories about gods, goddesses, heroes, strange creatures, and the origins of the civilization of ancient Greece. For hundreds of years before they were first written down, the stories were told and retold orally by the ancient Greeks. The tales were passed down over generations and are still known today as myths and legends.

Questions for Discussion

1. How does Ares use violence to try and solve his problems? Give at least two examples. Does this strategy work out well for him? Why or why not?

2. Ares is one of the twelve supreme gods of ancient Greece who lived on Mount Olympus. How is this an advantage for Ares? Are there any disadvantages?

3. What fact about Ares is your favorite? Explain why.

Writing Activity

Imagine you are an ancient Greek god and an enemy of Ares. Describe the special powers, weapons, and tools you have that might allow you to defeat him. Then, tell the story of an epic battle between you and the god of war. Who is victorious? Explain why.

About the Author

Thomas Kingsley Troupe is the author of over 200 books for young readers. When he's not writing, he enjoys reading, playing video games, and investigating haunted places with the Twin Cities Paranormal Society. Otherwise, he's probably taking a nap or something. Thomas lives in Woodbury, Minnesota, with his two sons.

About the Illustrator

Felishia Henditirto was born in Bandung, Indonesia, and has been fascinated by art and stories since she was a child. When everybody else in class was busy taking notes, she was stuck in her own world, drawing. She always has a thirst for magic and tries to find it in everything she does, especially in reading! If she is not working, you can find her visiting far, faraway places in the pages of a book.

Written by: Thomas Kingsley Troupe
Illustrated by: Felishia Henditirto
Design by: Under the Oaks Media
Series Development: James Earley
Editor: Kim Thompson

Library of Congress PCN Data
I Am Ares! / Thomas Kingsley Troupe
Greek Gods and Goddesses
ISBN 979-8-8873-5932-8 (hard cover)
ISBN 979-8-8873-5971-7 (paperback)
ISBN 979-8-8904-2030-5 (EPUB)
ISBN 979-8-8904-2089-3 (eBook)
Library of Congress Control Number: 2023912374

Printed in the United States of America.

Seahorse Publishing Company

www.seahorsepub.com

Published in the United States
Seahorse Publishing
PO Box 771325
Coral Springs, FL 33077